Headspace

I didn't start writing with intention to share my thoughts, I started writing to escape from myself and to put it all out there but in a closed space. I first began writing before my grandmother passed away and I would share my poems with her here and there, I continued but stopped as I got older. Recently, writing has again become my outlet. I found myself beginning to write when I felt like my feelings and thoughts wouldn't be received well by the person(s) they were directed to or anyone else for that matter. Today, I have gotten to a point where I want to share what is going on in my head, because I know that I am not the only person having feelings, or who may be hung up on a guy (or girl, whatever your preference is), afraid of what the future holds, or who is still dealing with issues from the past. The name Headspace is so fitting because that is exactly what this is, everything I write depends on the headspace I'm in at that particular moment and sometimes I can't escape. I hope that I am relatable and inspiring, and maybe you can get in or out of your headspace too.

The poems in Headspace are not in any chronological order, these are depictions of my feelings at any given time. Dates are my way of solidifying these in time. There are three categories: hurting, horny, and healing which represent my main three moods when I begin to write and immerse myself in what I am feeling.

HURTING

Puffy eyes, long days, tears falling, not much left to say.
Angry at yourself, angry at someone else. Be hurt, bask in it.

July 27

If this is going to bring us pain

I don't want to know anything

not even your last name

Let alone take it for my own

rid myself of my born identity

thinking our paths coincide

making plans that involve flowers and lace

because what I thought was love

wasn't sent from God himself

See I know that He said love never fails

so what we had wasn't true

but then I still disobey

afraid that I can't survive in my world

without you.

Robbed me of my energy

because you wanted more time to play

never thought about if I needed it

for a bad day

or to deal with your countless excuses

as to why you couldn't stay

Shame on me

willingly blaming myself because maybe

I wasn't enough

maybe

I didn't look like her

or my hair didn't fall like hers

my curves didn't curve like hers

shame on you for maximizing

my insecurities

instead of reassuring me that I was

beauty personified

I was a gem

pawned off over and over again

I accepted it as fate

knew you were unattainable

so I wanted to be the one to tame you

an animal yet you are

preying on me

because my defense was weak

blinded by what I thought it was

or what it could be

Shame on you

shame on me.

Maybe my favorite color should be green

as I radiate with envy of you

hanging back

as you get to experience the supernatural

the total consummation of energies

the end all be all

Jealous I am because I'm...

out of touch with the spiritual

cut off from the emotional

fighting for a spot in the physical

and mourning

over the mental

I am excluded from the group

I just get to gaze at what could be

never receiving a chance

to engage fully.

April 11

But nothing is ever really ours is it

see we tricked ourselves

thinking

we have possession over each other

You do what you do

and I'll

do my own thing

Nothing can really yolk us

not even that wedding ring

it's just a piece of metal

and I find no peace

meddling in the promise

of forever

because that far

I can't see.

August 9

We've disintegrated into "friends"

but when someone says your name around me

I cringe

not from any anger or mal intent

just because after all we went through

this is what it came to

Hearing about your accomplishments

second hand

seems weird to me

I used to get a text or call to confirm

you were the person I always knew you'd be

now as I scroll

I see pics

double tap but no comment

kinda like when I see you in public

surface level shit.

February 12

They say the saddest people

don't know what they want

I'm sad.

March 25

An icebreaker question

what's the craziest thing you've ever done?

My answer always differs

but I think I've found the one

falling in love

may be the wildest shit ever

because who knew

that for you

I'd never undo this tether

I'd always chase this high

and stay up late

considering the "why's"

put you before myself

look in the mirror

and lie

and practice this repeatedly

I think this is what they call insanity

funny because it's comfortable

well

until it goes wrong and humbles you

but never humble enough

right?

we always chase that high.

HORNY

Skin to skin, sweat dripping, thrill seeking, in and out of

positions. Climax chasing, back breaking, legs shaking. You

get the point...

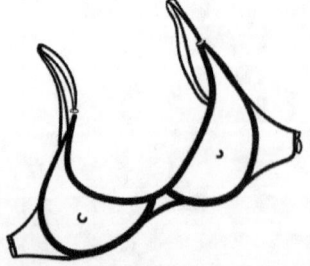

March 15

It's easier to wrap my legs around you

than my head around you

the latter comes with water

as it gathers in my eyes

wondering why we can't get it right

but in the bedroom it's all vibes

the kind that came with climaxes

as we reach our pivotal point

I would like to understand you

but right now

our bodies are joined

and not in the way that I long for

more so in the way

that I moan for

that temporary joy

but not many words follow

because if they did

they would consist of fear and regret

and why put that in the air

when the room still oozed with us

evidence of our ecstasy

thrown on the floor

similar to our regard

for one another's feelings

avoiding conversations

that could lead us to healing

we wouldn't dare do that

because we need a reason

to keep coming back.

Tell me

has another woman stroked your ego

this much lately?

I'm not trying to get deep into it

I just want to feel good

forget about the consequences

mascara running

making lines in my face

I knew all I needed was a taste

This isn't really penetrating more than the physical

I'm just trying to keep yelling your name

over the sound waves

Be quiet while the stereo plays

tell me it's all mine when you hold me

I don't care if it's a lie

I know we ain't that serious

just keep lying to me,

I'm going home in a few minutes.

Wake up right next to me

I'm emotionally drained

I just gave you

whatever was left of me

no need to worry about where we will take this

I'm not in the field of looking for relationships

It's me

not you

so don't get offended

I'm sure you're the light to someone's day

but I'm enjoying what's left of my shade

thank you for the moment

I live for times like this

exchanging energies

and in the morning

you leave

not to sound harsh or detached

I'm just in the process of getting my heart back.

March 4

Can I come over?

channeling my inner Aaliyah

can't lie

it's been awhile since I seen ya

been two seconds and you already read my text

you say yes

guess I'm not the only one

feeling the stress

I say let's relieve each other

of course you agree because all those rules

you have don't apply to me

I've always known that

Walk-in and Wi-Fi automatically connects

I've been here before

no need to knock

I have the code to the door

You grab me

my keys drop to the floor

nostalgia rushes over us

upstairs we go

and all our worries leave us soon

take me to the moon

you are more than capable

take me, I'm ready

willing and able.

July 23

I had a dream you spent the night

we were in and out of positions

while our shadows chased the light

candles flickered

in the near distance

warming up all of our ill-intentions

liquor reducing our inhibitions

because

we're going to do what we want

but what is that exactly?

It's giving each other the feeling

of relief,

we so desperately need.

Let's just say it was closure

let's say we needed to say goodbye

we can blame it on our feelings

and needing the answers to the "why's"

we can blame it on our chemistry

how our formulas appear to be

the same

how combining these substances

always leads to me calling your name

we can blame it on whatever

just as long as you're here with me

my hands on your head

keeping the position steady

we can blame it on lust

because that's surely what this is

let's just blame it on something

that'll allow us to get naked.

March 14

It's as simple as one, two

being around you

leaves no room for imagination

we need to feel the real thing

because we know the depths

we tend to go

not just physically

but being consumed in the emotional

which leads to me being consumed

by you

I take it all in as I start to breathe slow

looking at you with that smile

makes me want to stay here for awhile

let's take our time

let's drag this out please

because we know where too many of these moments

will lead

but for now

just look at me.

HEALING

These are the brighter days that they told me would come.

You are the template

the foundation

the skeleton of what I need

you are the cells

the carbon copy

of my expectations.

I'm in awe

of how raw you feel

skin to skin

we don't have to pretend

because it is what it feels like

I can laugh with you today

because you've experienced my night.

Oh how lucky we are

and even if this doesn't go far

I appreciate the time.

I find refuge in you

I never really wanted to

it just happened.

Here we are

grey doesn't even define us anymore

and I'm starting to feel unsure

but I'll fight it

the way my feelings fall out of me

and onto you

is astonishing

I get so caught up in your love

that I forget about how this has only been

a few months

but in the back of my mind

I hear your disregard for time

because it don't mean shit right?

Is it too early for a sentimental text?

because I can't stop singing Aaliyah's

"At your best"

I tell you, you are loved

and I mean every word

even at your worst

those eight letters will still ring true

because if I only love you at your best

does that sentence really have any value?

I don't think it was malicious

I think you had some demons

and didn't know how to fix it

I think that falling in love

put you in an awful position

because how could you maneuver

knowing your past wasn't dealt with

I don't hold it against you

it takes everything in me

but somehow

I still love you

I often think of what'd I'd say to you

like if you said you still loved me

would that be enough for me to untie

my emotional noose?

I guess the grey of the unknown is killing me

but remember

we never did well in that type of light anyway

I always needed our hue to be identifiable

and you were okay accepting the grey

something I always looked up to.

October 15

You make me feel...

natural, grandiose

like I'm still loved

even when I do the most

like I can still get a hug

after going ghost

Like what we feel is genuine, not for show

real, substantial

like I can dream as big as the ocean

like my intensity is noticed

like when I'm gone for a while

not a moment has been missed

Emotional, appreciated

like my opinion still matters

even when it's jaded

like I can say what I want even if you hate it

like I can be my complete self

and never have to fake it.

November 27

Some bridges I burn on purpose

I'm not talking cutting ties

just on the surface

I'm talking

leaving you on read when you're "hurting"

knowing the heartfelt reply ain't worth it

I know people are temporary and seasonal

they come in your life for specific reasons so,

learn to let go

whenever you see fit

don't stick around hoping to change them

they were probably in your life

to help you change yourself

because if you don't love you

don't assume someone else does.

www.ingramcontent.com/pod-product-compliance
Lightning Source LLC
Chambersburg PA
CBHW051347020726
47501CB00007B/2313